# Dip into Oneness

Beyond Knower, Known and Knowing

## Also by Sirshree

### Spiritual Masterpieces
### Self Realisation books for serious seekers

1. **The Magic of Awakening :** 111 Answers on Life and Living
2. **The Unshaken Mind :** Discovering the Purpose, Power and Potential of your mind
3. **Complete Meditation - 222 Questions :** From doing Meditation to being Meditation
4. **The Complete Meditator :** The Definitive Source Book for Complete Meditation
5. **The Supreme Quest :** Your search for the Truth ends there where you are
6. **Enlightenment :** Experience the Self Now!
7. **Self Enquiry :** With Understanding
8. **The Greatest Freedom :** Discover the key to an Awakened Living

### Self Help Treasures
### Self Development books for success seekers

9. **Inner Ninety Hidden Infinity :** How to build your book of values
10. **Inner 90 for Youth :** The secret of reaching and staying at the peak of success
10. **The Source for Youth :** You have the power to change your life
11. **Inner Magic :** The Power of self-talk
12. **Self Encounter :** The Complete Path - Self Development to Self Realization
13. **The Spirit of New :** Ten Thinking Approaches to bring a new turn in your life
14. **Invisible Confidence Visible Faith :** Gain Self Confidence and Release Faith
15. **The Five Supreme Secrets of Life :** Unveiling the Ways to Attain Wealth, Love and God

### New Age Nuggets
### Practical books on applied spirituality and self help

16. **The Source :** Power of Happy Thoughts
17. **Secret of Happiness :** Instant Happiness - Here and Now!
18. **Excuse me God... :** Fulfilling your wishes through the Power of Prayer and Seed of Faith
20. **Tea for Thoughts :** Take a spiritual break to dive deep within
21. **Help God to Help You :** Whatever you do, do it with a smile
22. **Freedom From Fear, Worry, Anger :** How to be cool, calm and courageous
23. **365 Happy Quotes :** Daily Inspirations from Sirshree
24. **Ultimate Purpose of Success:** Achieving Success in all five aspects of life
25. **The Unshaken Flame of Peace :** 10 Master Peace Solutions for creating a Powerful Life and a Prosperous World

### Profound Parables
### Fiction books containing profound truths

26. **Beyond Life :** Insights on Living, Growing and Dying
27. **The One Above :** What if God was your neighbour?
28. **The Warrior's Mirror :** The Path To Peace
29. **Master of Siddhartha :** Revealing the Truth of Life and Afterlife
30. **Put Stress to Rest :** Utilizing Stress to Make Progress
31. **Get Hired by God :** Inspiration at Work

## Dip into Oneness

By Sirshree Tejparkhi

© Tejgyan Global Foundation, 2015.

All Rights Reserved.

Tejgyan Global Foundation is a charitable organization with its headquarters in Pune, India.

First Edition : September 2015

Publisher : WOW Publishings Pvt. Ltd., Pune

---

Copyrights are reserved with Tejgyan Global Foundation and publishing rights are vested exclusively with WOW Publishings Pvt. Ltd. This book is sold subject to the condition that it shall not by way of trade or otherwise, be lent, resold, hired out, or otherwise circulated without the publisher's prior written consent in any form of binding or cover other than that in which it is published and without a similar condition including this condition being imposed on the subsequent purchaser and without limiting the rights under copyright reserved above, no part of this publication may be reproduced, stored in or introduced into a retrieval system, or transmitted, in any form, or by any means, electronic, mechanical, photocopying, recording or otherwise, without the prior written permission of both the copyright owner and the above-mentioned publisher of this book. Any person who does any unauthorized act in relation to this publication may be liable to criminal prosecution and civil claims for damages.

## *Preface*

# *Experience the Unknowable*

A person who uses eyeglasses cannot find them one day. He searches for his eyeglasses all around. When he is asked, "Where have you searched for your glasses?" he says, "I have searched the drawers, the cupboards, in every corner." He is then asked, "Are you sure you have properly searched everywhere?" He replies, "Yes, of course! I told you that I have carefully searched everywhere." When he is asked, "Can you see anything without your glasses?" he says, "No. I can't."

Do you see the folly in his seeking? He is able to search because he has already put on his eyeglasses! He already possesses what he is searching for. In order to remind him that he already has what he is searching for, he is continuously asked whether he is able to see properly. When he keeps replying in the affirmative, there is a chance that the truth may dawn upon him – he is already seeing through his glasses.

This is also true with the pursuit of the ultimate truth. The experience of Oneness, God, Consciousness, Divinity, Self, Christ, Allah (you may use any name) is already present here and now. We only need to shift our perspective. The ultimate truth exists beyond the realm of the human mind. It is constantly available, and yet, it is veiled. Just as the sun becomes invisible when shrouded by clouds, similarly the eternal truth becomes invisible, being masked by the mind.

*Truth cannot be attained by seeking; yet, only seekers have attained it!*

*When the seeker disappears in its pursuit, Truth reveals itself.*

The true pursuit of Oneness ends when the one who seeks, disappears! When the one, who is seeking, dives into the expanse of nothingness, he loses himself. This nothingness is not the dull void that the mind may imagine. It is the nothingness pregnant with the potential of everything. It reveals itself as a dynamic stillness which is the source of the vibrant dance of the universe, the very origin of life itself. It is a peaceful stillness, which gives rise to music and dance, dynamism and productivity.

Self-realization is the experience of the real 'I', the universal Self, which transcends all concepts, names and forms. It is the realization of our oneness with pure consciousness through direct experience of our true nature. There are many who experience momentary flashes of oneness when they are with nature or even in the midst of their daily lives. These are only *samples* of the experience of Self-realization.

However, the journey should not stop with mere glimpses. The real purpose of life is to stabilize in the experience of Self, to permanently abide in the experience of Self and express divine qualities of unconditional love, boundless bliss and peaceful stillness through the human body. Self-realization is incomplete, unless one attains Self-stabilization, followed by Self-expression. A true Guru is the one who leads the seeker beyond mere glimpses of Self-realization to stabilize permanently in the sublime bliss of Pure Consciousness.

Pure Consciousness precedes thinking and doing. It is timeless, space-less, limitless, all pervading and the very source of all life. It is the one who knows; the one who lives; the one who creates and enjoys the world. It is the Self that lives, experiences and expresses through each one of us.

The primary aim of human life is to awaken to the experience of Self, to abide in it, and cause others to awaken to the magnificent wellspring of Self within them. Anything that serves this purpose alone is worth engaging in.

May you attain the whole and sole purpose of life!

~ **Sirshree**

## *Editor's note*

This book is intended to assist seekers in their journey of truth. It is a translated English rendering of answers given by Sirshree in Hindi language to questions raised by disciples.

These are indeed profound answers to shallow questions. The questions arise from ignorance, but the answers arise from the quintessence of wisdom, from the heart. When Sirshree answers, he explains subtle aspects that raise the perspectives of the seekers.

Ultimate truth is unknowable. It can only be experienced with the help of right understanding. This understanding is beyond knowledge, in the realm of pure experience. Sirshree has coined the term 'Knowlerience' to represent this pure non-conceptual experience.

Sirshree delivers the subtlest understanding through casual contemporary language by weaving the highest aspects of the Truth into analogies (metaphors). It is this understanding that Sirshree imparts through the Magic of Awakening Retreat

(MA Retreat), where the direct experience of Self-realization and guidance to Self-stabilization are imparted. Details of the retreat are provided at the end of this pocket book.

It is suggested that the questions and their answers be read in the presented sequence as each answer leads to the subsequent question, thereby providing a logical flow, unraveling the deepest truth of Knowlerience beyond Knower, Known and Knowing.

No matter how many times you read these answers, each reading will cause you to awaken to a deeper aspect of yourself. As you read these answers, some insights will emerge. Some answers might lead you to a state of deep inner stillness. You may take a pause to dwell in stillness, and then continue reading.

If there are answers that you do not understand initially, park them aside for a while and move onto the following question. After reading the entire book, you may revisit those questions. They may make more sense to you then.

While care has been taken to try and preserve the intent, tone and depth of Sirshree's message, it is not possible to fully and accurately translate the deeper meaning and spirit of the discourse. The language may deviate from English grammatical norms at certain places. It is our humble request to pardon any such deviations.

~ **The Editorial team**

# *Answers that Awaken*

**Disciple :** When I was walking around the Ashram, I was spellbound by the beauty of the lush green hills. It was as if I am one with everything around me. Is this Self-realization?

**Sirshree :** First, it is important to clarify the understanding of Self-realization. A seeker may experience a deeply profound meditative state where he experiences a thoughtless state for quite some time. It is an experience of Self-realization. Someone may experience oneness with everything when he is on a nature trail. He experiences that he is no longer a separate entity. It is an experience of Self-realization. However, Self-realization is just the beginning. Self-stabilization is the goal. With Self-stabilization, the judging and comparing mind does not emerge thereafter.

**Disciple : What exactly happens with Self-realization?**

**Sirshree :** The state of Self-in-Rest is when the world is not created – an unexpressed state where Self alone exists. It is the original state where Shiva alone exists, where only subject exists. The experiencer is present, but cannot experience itself.

When there is only one without another, one cannot know himself. It is only when there is 'another' that one can sense one's own presence. Self-in-Rest gives rise to the state of Self-in-Action… the expression of Self. Shiva creates Shakti… subject creates object to experience itself. When Self manifests as the mind comprising thoughts, it is the state of Self-in-Action. Self experiences itself through expression. You use a mirror to see yourself, to know how you are. In the same way, the world is the expression of Self-in-Action. It serves like a mirror for Self to experience itself.

When Self gets identified with the mind, it gives rise to an illusion of 'many'. It projects a world, the knower of the world, and the act of knowing the world. Thus, the illusion of 'many' is born as Self assumes a separate individual identity for itself.

However, this assumed individual identity is merely a projection, an illusion. By being identified with this illusion, Self assumes itself to be the a separate knower of a world. It assumes an identity of a fictitious individual mind, that is knowing a separate "external" world. Thus, the knower of the world becomes separate from the known. The real purpose of this expression – the purpose of experiencing Self's own presence – is forgotten.

When Self begins to detach and dis-identify from this illusion with the right understanding, Self-witnessing gains importance over witnessing the world. The term 'Self-witness' is pivotal here, because the word 'witness' has been liberally used in spirituality, due to which people have remained stuck with the concept of 'witnessing'.

The ultimate purpose is not realized until there is a permanent shift from 'witness' to 'Self-witness'. While looking in a mirror, if you do not see yourself, then the purpose of the mirror is not served. In the same way, when the world of forms and phenomena is being witnessed, the focus should shift to Self who witnesses itself by using the world as a mirror.

When one stabilizes in the experience of Self-realization, the conviction about non-existence or falsehood of the 'fictitious separate individual' is established. The original nature of Self is recognized. Self continues to be in action and yet remains dis-identified from the mind-body.

Self-realization is when the ultimate purpose of Self behind creating this world is realized... when the real-'I' is realized.

**Disciple : What is the difference between Self-realization and Self-stabilization?**

**Sirshree :** Self-realization is the direct experience of Self. Self-stabilization comes when one abides permanently in the experience of Self. It is necessary to internalize the understanding completely to be stabilized in Self. When the wattage of a bulb is low, it cannot handle the electric current. If the bulb has to receive electricity, it is necessary to raise its wattage capacity.

So it is with the human body-mind. The bulb represents the human body-mind. When the understanding of Truth dawns for the first time in a human body-mind, it can be called Self-realization. However, to hold onto that Truth permanently, it is essential to raise the capacity of the body-mind. The state of Self-stabilization can emerge when the capacity of the body-mind is raised. One becomes established in the experience of Self.

The main obstacles in attaining Self-stabilization are the inappropriate tendencies present in that body-mind. It is due to these tendencies that the body-mind is not able to hold the Truth at all times. Even if a single tendency remains in the body-mind, it will pull that body-mind away from Truth. It is essential to get rid of these tendencies of the body-mind. When you work on getting rid of these tendencies, the state of Self-stabilization will emerge all by itself.

First, live in the present. When you are in the present, the tendencies of the body-mind can come to light and dissolve.

**Disciple : My thoughts keep wandering into the past. I regret my past decisions. How can I train my mind to live in the present?**

**Sirshree :** When the mind drops, you are in the present, in timeless existence. Initially this can be grasped only in external terms. For example, when you used to play a game, say football. Suppose you injured the foot which started bleeding. You would play for an hour and won't realize that it is injured. You won't sense the pain. It is only when someone else notices and tells you, "Hey... your foot is bleeding" that you would start sensing the pain. The pain was not being felt earlier because the mind had dropped while playing.

Similarly, when someone plays the piano, he is lost when the performance is at its peak. He does not exist then. The performer is lost in the performance. All that remains is the performance. Where is the mind when this is happening? It has dropped for some time. But the mind comes back later and claims that it was present during the performance. And to top that, the mind even takes credit for having been the performer. See this illusion!

Musicians love to be lost in the peak of their performance. Athletes like being in the thick of activity. The real joy that they experience is because they experience the present moment as the mind drops. However, they do so without the right understanding. They believe that it is the music performance or the athletic activity that is giving them joy. The source of joy is not in the gross external world. Without this understanding, they continue to seek the joy of the present moment in external pursuits.

What is the mind? It is nothing else but thoughts. The present moment is always happening. If you are checking whether you are in the present moment, you are trying to capture the present moment in your thoughts. There is no need to try and grasp the present moment in your thoughts.

The mind insists, "I want to grasp the present moment; I want to know how it is like." This wish becomes a hurdle in just being in the present. When you attempt to capture the present moment in your thoughts, it eludes you. You can either think about the present moment, or just *be* in the present.

The past is memory; future is imagination. Past and future exist only in thoughts that arise in the present moment. Hence, the mind believes that the present can be understood in thoughts, just like past or future. When the mind drops, you experience the timeless eternal present, without the notion of past or future.

**Disciple : Can I experience Self if I am in the present?**

**Sirshree :** The question of relevance is: who is aspiring for the experience of Self? Is the mind going to experience it? This is like someone who attends a music concert and starts rubbing his eyes because he cannot hear the music. He needs to understand that listening to music or any sound in general has nothing to do with eyes. Something must be wrong with his ears. But he believes that music can be seen with eyes!

In the same way, when the mind says that I want to experience Self, it is like eyes that wish to *see* music. The experience of Self is constantly ongoing. When the mind is infused with this understanding, it surrenders its insistence to experience Self. As the mind is prepared to surrender, the desire to experience Self is dropped. The mind becomes still, non-existent as it were.

So when thoughts are absent, is it that there is no one? Even in the absence of thoughts there is a knowing that is happening. With practice, the mind becomes still, making it conducive for Self to return onto Self experience. Then the real experiencer experiences the experiencer through every experience.

**Disciple : You say that knowing happens without thoughts. But we have to think to know anything. We**

know about anything through our thoughts.

**Sirshree:** Presence comes first; thinking comes later. To think, you have to first *be*. Presence is your true nature. Presence by itself cannot be experienced without being aware. The awareness of existence is the essence of Presence. Presence is the most obvious truth about you.

Yet, presence is lost in the constant chatter of thoughts. Thinking cannot lead to the experience of presence. To experience presence, we need to be aware of what *is*.

Descartes, the Greek philosopher, had said, "I think, therefore I am". However, if existence were dependent on thinking, then you would not exist if you were to stop thinking. This is certainly not the case. When you are in deep sleep, you do not think. And yet, you do exist. You may even comment on waking that you slept well. You have to exist during deep sleep to be able to know that you did sleep well.

Presence is independent of thought. Presence just *is*. Your sense of presence is the simple truth that you are constantly and spontaneously aware of. This knowing is beyond thoughts. It is because you are present that you engage activity. "I am reading this book." "I am" comes first. It is because "I am" that "I am reading." And "I am aware that I am reading."

You tend to be lost in whatever follows 'I am…' I am a man, I am reading, I am smart, I am sad, I am an artist. Everything that follows 'I am' is subject to change. But the 'I am' is constant. It is the constant sense of presence that enlivens all activities of life.

Presence is the most obvious experience. It is the open secret – so open and obvious that you easily fail to notice it. The sense of presence has been unbroken ever since your body was born. You may change your identity – from being a child to becoming an adolescent, from being a youth to a middle-aged family maker, from being a student to one who earns a living, from being a parent to being a grandparent. However, the sense of presence remains unchanged; it remains constant. If you were to take away all the roles that you consider to be 'you', you would still exist.

So the awareness of presence precludes thinking. You need not think in order to know. Knowing through thoughts is information. Knowing beyond thoughts is direct experience. It is a different kind of knowing. The mind, which is nothing but thoughts, is not the knower. The knower of thoughts is the real knower. The real knower exists beyond the mind, beyond the world.

**Disciple : How can I experience the real knower without thoughts?**

**Sirshree :** With alert observation, you will see that there are three elements. These three elements can be expressed in words as the "seer, scene and seeing". Imagine an onlooker witnessing a scene. The act of seeing is happening between the seer and the scene. With awareness, it can be known that the three elements (seer, scene, and the act of seeing) are one in essence.

Understand this carefully. Who exactly is the knower of the "seer, scene, and seeing"? Perform an exercise to understand this. [*Experiment adapted for readers.*] For a minute, take a pause and observe this page... notice the outline of this page... the colour of the paper... the feel of holding the book in your hands... Observe your hands holding the book... See how the reading of these lines is happening.

And now, right now, notice how the observation is taking place. Feel the presence of the eyes that now see the book... The eyes are watching the page. Notice the feelings and thoughts that arise as the book is being observed. Now... who is knowing these eyes, these feelings, these thoughts? Who is knowing that the reading is happening? From where are these being known? Notice that all these are also being known at a subtler level. We will now stop this exercise.

What do we understand from this exercise? There are three elements involved right now even as you continue reading – this book is the "scene", the mind that reads through the eyes and dwells in feelings is the "seer" of the book, and the act of reading is happening. However, the knower who stands apart distinctly from "seer, scene and seeing" is also present.

The mind becomes the seer (subject) and witnesses the scene (object). But what enlivens these three? In whose presence do these three come alive? Who is actually knowing all thes "seer, scene, and seeing"? The real knower is the Self that exists beyond the mind.

**Disciple :** I did not understand. You said that the "seer, scene and seeing" are one. They are also being known. How can the knower be different from the seer?

**Sirshree :** The seer, scene, and the act of seeing are stacked together like the slices that make a sandwich. You prepare a sandwich by stacking slices of bread with some toppings or butter between them. You then press the slices together to make the sandwich.

Just as you prepared the sandwich to enjoy eating it, the Self has created the sandwich of "seer, scene and the act of seeing" to enjoy **knowing itself.** Just as you are separate from the sandwich that you eat, Self is separate from this sandwich. When this sandwich of seer, scene and seeing is witnessed with the eye of wisdom, their underlying oneness can be known. The sandwich then serves as a mirror for the Self to know itself.

Self (Consciousness, God) is the ultimate knower. Self is ever aware. When Self gets attached and identified with the mind (seer), the underlying oneness of these "seer, scene, and seeing" is lost. Self forgets its real identity by being lost in the details of these three. Due to this entanglement, the Self assumes itself to be an individual mind. The individual mind believes itself to be separate from everything else. It assumes a limited existence, instead of being one with totality. This false assumption is called ego. Thus, the mind that lacks wisdom becomes an obstacle in seeing the oneness of the "seer, scene, and seeing". You may also call it "knower, known and knowing".

**Disciple : So the mind is assumed to be the separate knower. As a result the Self cannot experience itself.**

**Sirshree :** Yes. Let us understand this through an example. When you keep an iron rod in fire it becomes red hot. If you bring anything in contact with this red hot iron rod, it acts like fire. The iron rod assumes the role of fire. But the heat held by the iron rod is not original. It is borrowed.

Similarly, the mind borrows the witnessing potential, the witnessing ability, from Self and becomes a false witness. This drama of the false witness goes on for some time. Eventually, the mind has to fall back on Self when it is exhausted of this potential, to be replenished. This replenishment, this rejuvenation occurs in deep sleep. Then it wakes up after sleep and again assumes the role of seer. When the mind assumes a separate identity of a witness, the "seer, scene and seeing" appear separate. For Self-experience, it is essential that the "seer, scene and seeing" should be sandwiched as one. For this, the mind has to drop.

**Disciple : From what you said, I understand that Self experiences Self through the medium of a sandwich made of the seer, the scene, and the act of seeing. Is this "Self-in-Rest" or "Self-in-Action"?**

**Sirshree :** It is the experience of Self-in-Rest. The action happening in the form of "seer, scene and seeing" creates this phenomenal world. Self-in-Rest uses whatever has been created as a mirror to experience itself. It is important to experience "seer, seen and seeing" as One.

Otherwise, when the three are experienced as separate elements, Self forgets its original nature. The mind assumes the role of a false subject and considers the **seemingly** separate world as the scene, the object. The mind claims, "I can see this... I am seeing that..." It tries to take credit for experiences. Self-in-Rest is just present; it just exists. It does not need to stake any claim!

The real purpose is to sense the presence, to experience existence, to be aware of pure awareness itself. This purpose is not being served. The mind derives energy from Self to assume the role of seer. Self is the original seer. Let the three be sandwiched into one instead of the fragmented perspective of a separate seer and scene.

In a laboratory, the mind observes the equipment placed on the laboratory table. It becomes the knower of everything in the laboratory. However, from the standpoint of Self, the mind itself is placed on the laboratory table. The mind and the world, together, become the object! The Self is the ultimate knower.

**Disciple : How does Self manifest the phenomenal world? Is there any scientific basis for the existence of the ultimate knower?**

**Sirshree :** The experience of Self does not need any evidence. Presence is self-evident. It is the mind that seeks evidences in terms of what it already knows. Even so, revelations from research in the field of quantum physics have revolutionized the scientific perspective of the essence of wholeness and the illusion of matter.

Quantum physicists discovered that physical atoms are made of spinning energy. Theoretically speaking, if you were to observe the composition of an actual atom, what would you see? From a distance, the atom would appear like a translucent sphere. As you go nearer, you find that the atom is empty. The atom disappears! What appeared as the structure of the atom turns out to be physical emptiness when you scrutinize it.

It turns out that atoms are made of invisible energy, not tangible matter. It then appears that all material substance in the universe is actually energy vibrating in physical emptiness.

Further, quantum physicists inferred that matter could be simultaneously defined as a material particle as well as an immaterial energy field – a wave. This is what the physicist Albert Einstein realized and concluded with his famous equation: $E = mc^2$. Energy and matter are one and the same. Einstein discovered that the universe that we live in is not made up of discrete, material objects separated by space. The universe is one indivisible, dynamic whole. Energy and matter are aspects of the same underlying unified field.

Physicists performed an experiment of passing electrons through a double-slit. When an electron wave was made to pass through the double-slit and fall upon a photographic film, it created a pattern of striations, indicating wave-interference. This suggested that the electrons were behaving like waves (energy). However, when scientists tried to observe the path of the electron, they were baffled to find that it *chose* a particular slit, as if it were a particle!

When scientists attempted to watch electron behavior, the observed outcome of experiments was influenced by the assumptions and expectations of what they intended to observe. The scientists Neumann and Wagner have postulated their interpretation of experiments conducted by Heisenberg and Schrodinger.

They have proven that an observer actually modifies objective outcomes simply by the act of observation. In other words, we shape our world by the way we observe it. When not observed, everything exists as a field of infinite unexpressed possibilities, collapsing into a particular manifestation when observed.

The universe is being created and perpetuated due to witnessing by Self. The observer exists as the underlying field which transcends the manifested details. The observer field is like a screen projecting the material world upon itself, just like a movie is projected on a cinema screen.

**Disciple : Why does the observer get lost in the manifested world? And how does the observer return onto himself in the midst of this world?**

**Sirshree :** The universe is made of vibrations (waves). These vibrations are being brought about by the nature of Presence, of Self-in-Rest. It is like a dancer who begins to dance so fast that he cannot be clearly seen. All that is visible is the hazy expression of dance. One will not be able to appreciate the presence of the dancer as one is lost in the expression of dance. As one has not seen the dancer before the dance commenced, one remains stuck in the various aspects of the dance.

Similarly, there is the innate tendency to forget the original state of Self-in-Rest. Awareness drifts to the expression of Self-in-Action.

When awareness is trained to return onto Self, it becomes possible to clearly spot the dancer in and through every movement of the cosmic dance. In every experience, the focus will be on the dancer —Self-in-Rest—without whom the dance would not happen! At the same time, had it not been for the cosmic dance, the dancer would not be able to recognize his infinite potential! Without this dance of the manifest universe, the dancer –Self– would not get a chance to know its own magnifient nature.

**Disciple: Where is Self with respect to the world? Is Self within us? Does Self exist outside the world or does it permeate the world?**

**Sirshree :** It is difficult to capture the true nature of Self in words. When you learn that the experience of Self is constantly going on within you, you might imagine that Self exists within the human body. And, though technically or logically it may be considered true, Self is not just within the body. Rather, the body exists within Self. All of existence is happening within Self.

Think of a fish living in water. Water is the most obvious and all-pervading presence for the fish. It is the essential medium that keeps the fish alive. Water exists not only within the fish, but also all around it. Water is so close to its eyes that the fish doesn't realize that it is in water. What if the fish swam off in search of water, asking, "Where is water?"

This is precisely what even the questioning mind would ask when it is told about the all-pervading nature of consciousness: "Where is this consciousness? Is it within me, or elsewhere?"

The experience of presence or consciousness is so close to us; in fact, it is our very essence! If you carefully observe, you will find that the spatial concepts of *within* and *outside* belong in the realm of thoughts. From the standpoint of Self, there is neither *within* nor *outside*. We are inseparable beingness at the very core. Our living presence is the experience of Self.

*Inside* and *outside* are relative concepts used by the mind to conceive the sense of space. Self is outside of inside-and-outside. At the same time, Self is also inside of outside-and-inside. This answer may baffle the human intellect. The presence of Self cannot be conceptualized in thoughts.

**Disciple : From what you said, I understand that the question of "where" Self exists cannot be conceived by mind. But, can you please help me with this so that I get some sense of what it implies?**

**Sirshree :** You can understand this with the help of a picture. Visualize a painting in front of you. In this painting, there is a person standing and watching a kite flying in the sky. You will say that this person is the seer or subject. The flying kite in the sky is the scene or object. The person who is the seer and the kite which is the scene are inside the painting, on the canvas; but the painter is outside this painting. When you ask where is Self, it like the person inside the painting asking where the painter is. The painted can never know the painter!

In this example, the painter is depicting that a person is watching a kite in the sky. However, apart from the details of the painting, what is the painter achieving? He is glorifying the expression of art through his painting. This painter is knowing about himself, about his creative potential. "Who am I? What kind of a painter am I? I created the seer, I also created the scene, and the act of seeing is happening between them. Now I am getting to know about myself: why I fashion such kites. I am realizing why I bring forth such ideas on canvas." The creator of what is being expressed on the canvas of life, the knower of what is being fashioned on this living screen, exists outside the painting.

Whenever you look at a painting, you also know that your mind is observing the scene on the canvas. The mind which observes everything in this canvas of life is also actually placed on the canvas. The mind becomes a part of the painting. In other words, the real knower, who wishes to know himself, creates the seer and the scene, thereby fulfilling the purpose of knowing himself!

**Disciple : What is the relationship between Self and the scenes that are manifesting in life? Do the specific details of the scenes have anything to do with Self, or does it relate to the nature of the mind?**

**Sirshree :** If the earlier analogies have not served to explain this, then listen to yet another analogy which will clarify what is happening.

We all know of televisions that have a front screen. Imagine a television that has a screen at the rear side as well. You would never see such a television practically, but just imagine this for the purpose of this analogy. You may call this a dual-sided or double-screen television. Imagine that there is a torch placed behind this dual-sided television. Initially there is pitch darkness. Before the light falls on the rear-side screen, the television is switched off from both sides. When the torch is switched on, its light falls on the rear-side screen. What will happen when the light of the torch falls on the rear-screen? The light of the torch reflects back from the rear-screen and illuminates the torch itself.

Now, relate this analogy with what you have heard so far about Self-in-Rest and the mind. Self-in-Rest brings about the state of Self-in-Action with this auspicious wish that the light should reflect back and illuminate the source from where it originates. The torch itself is in darkness. You know that when the torch is lit in darkness, all objects other than the torch are illuminated. After lighting the torch, the light gets scattered but the torch does not get self-illuminated. The light of the torch lights up the space around it, but the torch itself remains in darkness.

When the torchlight strikes the rear-screen of the television, the torch does get self-illuminated by the reflected light. Additionally, the television also switches on, projecting several channels. Now, on the front screen, a serial is being telecast in which a person is narrating his life story. He says, "I had to go through so many difficult situations in my life, why did this happen with me?" Such scenes are being projected on the front screen.

In truth, the sole purpose of the light was to reflect back and illuminate the source of the light –the torch– itself. All these other happenings are just an additional bonus, a by-product. As a by-product, several such characters such as I, you, he, and she appear in this game of illusion or *maya*. These scenes are being manifest through the various channels on the front-screen. But they are just a by-product and not the real purpose.

**Disciple : What's the exact significance of the double-screen in the analogy?**

**Sirshree :** The significance of the double-screen TV is to indicate two screens – the front-screen represents the external world, the rear-screen represents the inner world, the world created within the mind. The external world is where the movie of life is going on. It may be a tragedy or a horror movie, a violent movie or a suspense thriller. It is the way life is manifesting and visible in the external world. This is symbolized by the programs being telecast on the front-screen.

The rear-screen represents whatever is being formed in the inner mind – various beliefs, preconceived notions, stories, assumptions, prejudices, and tendencies. This film is being played on the rear-screen. This rear-screen is used as a reflective medium, a mirror, for Self to experience Self. This analogy is useful in explaining how Self uses the world to experience Self.

Don't read more into this analogy than what it is meant to convey. If the TV had a rear-screen as well, then what would be the purpose of the rear-screen? It would be to reflect the projected light of the torch on the torch itself. When the rear-screen is able to perfectly reflect light on the source, then it also has a transformative effect on the programs being projected on the front-screen. This is how the quality of the rear-screen is related to the expression on the front-screen.

To the extent that the inner mind is cleansed off preconceived notions, beliefs, stories and tendencies, to that extent Self will be able to experience Self by using the mind and projected world as a mirror.

Self is the writer, producer, director, the hero, the villain and also the audience of the movie of life. The purpose of Self in making the movie is to experience itself by expressing its creative potential.

Self is projecting light on the rear-screen of the body-mind, thereby illuminating itself, being self-aware. The TV represents the human body-mind which is enlivened by the light of awareness. In the process, several different types of films are being projected due to the light of awareness that falls upon the body-mind. Somebody's film is an emotional drama or a tragedy. Someone else's film is a classical art film. Someone's film is dragging slowly at a snail's pace in which tears are flowing due to emotions. Someone's film is a horror film in which the person is always gripped with fear. For someone else, a comedy film is going on.

When Self-in-Rest experiences Self's own presence continually and never gets diverted from Self experience, then the body-mind will serve as a medium for the real expression of Self. Then the movie being projected on the front-screen into the world would express the standpoint of Self. For this, Self needs to be established in the conviction that there is only one whole and sole purpose behind creating the body-mind - Self should experience Self.

**Disciple : Is Self always self-illuminated through the light thrown back from the rear-screen? Is it already always happening as a default process?**

**Sirshree :** Understand the difference between "Presence" and "Sense of Presence". It is owing to Presence that the world exists. However, Presence is not aware of itself. Illumination is happening. However, complete Self-illumination happens only when the mind is pure and clean.

To the extent that the mind is cluttered and clouded, to that extent Self forgets its own presence in the entanglement of the mist created in the inner mind (the rear-screen). To the extent that the inner mind becomes pure, to that extent Self-illumination can occur, to that extent Self can know Self's presence and express divine qualities on the front-screen. It is for this purpose that *sadhana* (the practice of inner cleansing) is imparted.

Initially it becomes a necessary practice to seat the body in meditation with closed eyes. With the conviction that arises from recognition through practice, Self becomes increasingly aware of Self's pure presence.

When you try to imagine or conceive a "knower", understand that "knower" is also a concept of mind. There is no "knower". There is only "knowing", which is beyond subject and object, beyond the seer, the scene, and the act of seeing.

The quality of "Self-knowing through direct experience" is gifted to human being. Knowing the knower through the sense of Presence is possible through human existence. This is not possible in animals. In a lighter vein, it is good that animals do not have the aspect of being aware of knowing. Because, it is due to this gift that all the illusory entanglement also results as a by-product!

When one is able to see all the so-called problems of this world as a mere by-product of this gift of "knowing", then there is no problem whatsoever! Whatever is happening will be seen from a detached perspective without labels and used as a mirror to experience Self's presence.

**Disciple :** How can I develop this detached perspective whilst going through worldly activity?

**Sirshree :** All the affairs of the world happen in the presence of the sun. Flowers blossom in the presence of the sun. Human life is dependent on the sun. Man wakes up at sunrise and retires for the day after sunset. However, the sun does not wake anyone up, nor does it put anyone to sleep. The sun is merely present. All activities happen owing to the presence of the sun. In the same way, all work – including thinking – happens in the presence of who you truly are.

You are truly detached when Presence of Self becomes aware of itself, when "I am aware that I am", when consciousness becomes conscious of itself. It is about being present to the living presence, being aware of your pure undeniable existence. It is about being awake to the light that shines upon everything that is being known.

Experiencing the presence of Self through the medium of thoughts can also be understood as the second news. We always focus on the first news that our thoughts convey. Suppose a thought occurs: "It's such a lovely, bright sunny day!" While this is the content of the thought, it is actually also conveying the news that you are alive and awake. In other words, the second news is: "Consciousness exists", "I am". We usually get caught up with the first news and consequently the second essential news is lost.

As a daily practice, you can raise your awareness about the second news. You get flooded with various bits of information every minute. With every such input, you can remind yourself of the second news.

**Disciple :** How can I ignore important news and just live with the truth that Consciousness exists? After all, we need to live in a practical world!

**Sirshree :** See… this thought is also just another thought! Again, this thought too is conveying the news that Consciousness exists.

This does not mean that you should ignore the happenings of the world. Of course, you will heed them and take necessary action. However, everything that happens is an opportunity, an invitation to shift to the essential underlying truth –that Self (Consciousness) is enlivening all this. While you attend to and act upon the first news, you should shift to the second news.

Shift your attention from the body-mind to Consciousness. Turn back your attention from the objects of perception to that which enables you to perceive, from thought to that which enables you to think. You will then rise above the changing and limited to that which is changeless, eternal and boundless.

**Disciple :** Does identification with our thoughts and emotions affect Self-illumination and thereby the experience of Self? If the front screen is filled with thoughts or feelings of hatred or anger, then does the self-illumination of the torch (Self) reduce? Does the experience of Self increase when there are no thoughts?

**Sirshree :** Self-experience is happening constantly. There is nothing like an "increase" or "decrease" of Self-experience. The matter is only about being aware of Self experience; the awareness of Self-experience; knowing that knowing is happening. Self-experience neither increases nor decreases. The *awareness of* Self-experience may increase or decrease.

This can be understood, again, with the example of a TV which is switched on. The TV screen is lit up. However, in the afternoon, if the windows of the room are open to sunlight, then the TV screen will appear faint. Due to the brightness of sunlight in the room, you may not be able to clearly make out that the TV screen is lit-up. When windows are closed and curtains are drawn, then it may appear as if the TV screen has become brighter. But, you know that the TV screen is the same. It has not become brighter. It is just that you have become more aware that the screen is lit-up.

Similarly, Self experience is constant. It does not come and go; it does not increase or decrease. Awareness of Self experience may reduce or can rise.

**Disciple : Is it that the mind should be absent for Self to experience itself? Is a thoughtless state essential for this to happen?**

**Sirshree :** When Self identifies with thoughts, it leads to the notion of being a separate illusory individual. This becomes a hurdle in the experience of Self. During the process of disentangling, initially the stilling of the mind is conducive for Self in experiencing Self.

With practice comes conviction about Self's sense of presence. Once firm conviction is established, then it becomes irrelevant whether thoughts exist or not. With conviction, ignorance is dispelled and Self constantly abides in Self experience, regardless of the presence of absence of thoughts, feelings, and actions. With conviction about Self's presence, the illusory separate individual no longer exists. The thoughtless state of mind, or a relatively still mind definitely assists in building conviction in Self's presence. But it is not a prerequisite.

**Disciple : Can Self experience Self when the intuitive mind is functional?**

**Sirshree :** With the firm conviction of Self's sense of presence, the intuitive mind can continue to function. Worldly activities can continue to happen while Self experience is happening. It can be clerly seen that the limited false individual does not exist. All the so-called problems also cease to exist.

Problems appear as problems due to the skewed perspectives of the mind. When you go beyond the mind, then you go beyond perspectives. Then there is nothing that you can consider a problem! Everything is merely an aspect of the grand expression of Self, only serving as a mirror to know Self's own grandeur.

**Disciple : How do I shift to the standpoint of Self-in-Rest? Is there anything that I can practice to shift my standpoint?**

**Sirshree :** Again, the question to be asked is – who is aspiring to shift to the standpoint of Self-in-Rest? Who needs to go within to grasp the experience of Self? Is the mind going to experience it? No. The TV screen cannot know the torch. The TV screen only borrows the torchlight to project the various films.

When such questions arise, you need to follow it up with the question, "Who am I now?" This helps the real 'I' to detach from the mind and return to the source. The standpoint of Self, the standpoint of the screen on which films are being played is self-evident. The mind only needs to be still and the Self is revealed to itself.

When you understand the divine game of Self, you will begin to truly enjoy this comedy. Life is indeed a comedy, but who will tell whom that 'Only Self exists'. When you truly understand this through experience, then the real comedy film will commence. In such a film, the joyous laughter that emanates will spring from the heart.

Only Self exists. You need to investigate and find out whether the limited individual, which you assume yourself to be, truly exists. When this understanding deepens, you will attain the inner bliss of liberation. This understanding will give you ultimate joy. When such a divine film is played on the screen of your body-mind, then you will be able to fully experience its bliss.

**Disciple : I will try to practice inquiring "Who am I now?" in and through daily situations. I have heard about the practice of Self-inquiry where the seeker is made to investigate "Who am I." How does inquiring upon "Who am I now" exactly help?**

**Sirshree :** When an individual identity is assumed in thoughts, it gives birth to the notion of a separate 'I', confined within the boundaries of the human body. With the birth of this illusory separate 'I', whatever happens with the body-mind, seems to happen to a 'me', whatever belongs at the body-level becomes 'mine'.

Whatever is inside the skin becomes 'me' and everything else becomes 'not me'. You have been living this lie without questioning it, because you find everyone else around you living in the same illusion.

This illusion is complete when the flip-side of "I… me… mine" is also *imagined* into existence. Whatever is 'not me' becomes 'you… we… they… it'. This illusion is the root cause of all suffering, struggle and various defilements such as fear, anger, hatred, ill-will, and jealousy.

Forgetfulness of who we truly are leads to false identification with who we are not. We have become so addicted with the beliefs and stories that constitute our false personality that we continually try to improve and enrich our personality.

In the competitive world, personality is often used as a mask to flaunt who we are as individuals. But personality is actually a superficial outfit that can be changed. Working on personality doesn't cause any harm unless we believe that we *are* the personality. It is not difficult to notice that no matter how much we work on our personality, we lack the fulfillment of who we truly are.

The mind is a bundle of thoughts in which each thought is linked to a point of reference – the 'I'. No thought can exist without this point of reference. This point of reference called 'I' is a false notion that keeps changing every instant.

Consider an example to understand how the reference of 'I' keeps changing. Suppose one says:

*"My hand was wounded when I had been to the workshop. I was scared when I found that my hand was bleeding profusely. I then thought of visiting the doctor to dress up the wound."*

When one says, "I had been to the workshop", the word 'I' is being used to refer to the body. You keep saying many such things during the day by assuming yourself as the body. "I had food, I climbed the stairs, I laughed" etc. Here 'I' refers to the body.

The same sentence also says, *"My hand was wounded."* Whom does the 'My' refer to? If the earlier identification with the body were to be used, one would have said, "I was wounded." When you say, 'My hand was wounded', you consider yourself the owner of your body. It is only when you assume yourself as separate from "your" body that you can say 'My hand'. Thus, the point of reference for the 'I' has shifted from the body to the owner of the body in the same sentence.

When you say, *"I was scared"*, the 'I' in this context refers to the mind. The body cannot feel scared. The mind feels scared just as it also feels sad or elated, moody or ecstatic.

*"I thought of visiting the doctor."* Here again, the reference has shifted from the mind to the intellect. Thinking is considered an intellectual faculty. Here you assume yourself the intellect.

From this example, you can understand how the point of reference is false and how it keeps changing. The use of the words 'I', 'Me', 'Mine' differs in various contexts. This was an example of only three sentences.

Upon deeper contemplation, you will come across innumerable identities of 'I'. Different identities of 'I' spring into awareness at different points in time. However, due to delusion, you always believe it to be the same 'I'. Being lost in delusion, the real 'I' remains in the dark. Your true nature never gets an opportunity to shine forth as it is eclipsed by these false identities.

Clearing the cobwebs of this illusion requires rigorous and persistent Self-inquiry so that you're able to see all the facets of the mind. True inquiry serves the purpose of dismantling this daydream so that truth is revealed.

When you chose to spend time in stillness on a daily basis by focusing on the question "Who am I now?" you will be led to the experience of Self. Asking "Who am I now?" is one of the most powerful and effective ways of breaking out of this identification with the false 'I'.

**Disciple: There is a question that keeps nagging me. I was waiting to ask this. If this world is a divine expression of Self, then why is negativity a part of it? Why are people deceitful? Why doesn't goodness pervade this expression? Why is struggle there in life?**

**Sirshree:** Many people wonder why this world has been created. They question the very purpose of existence. Those who feel depressed complain about life. They blame an imaginary creator for creating the world in the way they perceive it. Some go even further to the extent of concluding that it would have been better if this world was never created. People often wonder: Why are some people deceitful, while others are honest? Why do some people sing melodiously, while others sing harshly? Why do some people appear beautiful or pleasant, while others appear ugly?

The missing link in their understanding is very subtle. If the creator had never created this phenomenal world, replete with its beautiful variety, if people who complain this way were never created, how would it ever be known whether creating the world was good or bad, whether it was useful or useless. Something has to exist first to know how it is. If nothing existed, there would be no question of knowing.

A painter mixes fundamental colours to create new colours. He creates many colours which also includes black. One may wonder why the painter has made a colour called 'black', as it is appears dark and depressing. However, for the painter, black is as important as any other colour. Thanks to black colour, he is able to lend depth to his art and give it a three-dimensional appearance. Black highlights and enhances the beauty of other colours by offering a contrast.

Some people sing harshly, but they are also important in the Creator's plan. If it were not for them, then those who sing melodiously won't be valued. Similarly, deceit fulfils its higher purpose of elevating the value of honesty. Struggle highlights the value of smoothness and ease. Everything that exists has its importance. The fact that they exist implies that they have a role to play in the higher scheme. But when we look at everything from a limited percpective, we develop preferences and get into the habit of comparison and judgment.

We need to understand the game being enacted in the universe. We need to understand our role in the cosmic scheme. When we complain, 'Why is this person behaving so strangely?', 'Why doesn't this man lead life as we do?' and so on, we are missing the higher perspective of life.

We need to think from the creator's point of view. What is the creative intention behind using these various colours and shades in life? Why create things that we label as 'bad'? The ultimate purpose is benevolent. The sole intention behind creation is to experience and express the highest creative potential. Where there are mountains, there are bound to be deep valleys. One cannot exist without the other. Black was created to enhance whiteness. Without black, can there be anything that we can distinguish as 'white'? Without the white background that pervades paper, you cannot recognize the black letters that are written on it. Such contrast has been created so as to transcend both polarities and experience the 'unknowable'.

**Disciple: Experience the unknowable? Can you please explain?**

**Sirshree:** Suppose that you are seated in a wide expanse of empty open space which extends infinitely in all directions. If someone were to say that this empty expanse is the pinnacle of creation, the highest creation. Would you believe it? Further, if you were told that this expanse of nothingness where you are seated is your home, would it make sense?

**Disciple:** It doesn't make logical sense.

**Sirshree:** It wouldn't, because this is beyond the comprehension of the intellect. It is beyond the imagination of the mind. Now, in that limitless expanse, suppose that four walls were introduced around you and you were then told that this is your home. Would you agree?

**Disciple:** Yes.

**Sirshree:** This is because now something has been 'created', the presence of which enables you to realize the vast expanse. Without these walls, the empty space did not make sense. Though you still exist in the same space as before, the walls serve the purpose of making you aware of that space.

In an absolute sense, thoughts –regardless of the content that they convey—are like the walls mentioned earlier. They are instrumental in experiencing the silence that exists in the background. If thoughts serve this purpose, then that is the highest creation.

In the same way, any creation –be it a thought, feeling, sound, object or event— is an essential limitation which is created only as an instrument to experience the limitless unknowable reality. The experience of the unknowable is the highest creation. True meditation reveals the experience of the unknowable.

**Disciple: From the standpoint that you have explained, what is true meditation?**

**Sirshree:** True meditation is not attention. Meditation is neither concentration nor contemplation. In India, the word '*Dhyan*' has come from spiritual scriptures. Spiritual seekers understood the deeper aspects of meditation. However, in today's world the meaning of meditation is misconstrued.

The words 'attention', 'contemplation' and 'meditation' have been used interchangeably. Therefore, the word meditation has lost its deeper significance.

Meditation is a quality of Self, an attribute of your essential nature. Meditation is the source which is ever present, regardless of whether we are in the state of deep sleep or in waking state.

The simple meaning of meditation is "doing nothing." However, some people find "doing nothing" very difficult. They try to *do* "nothing" instead of "doing nothing". They ask how it is possible to do "nothing". It is like asking, "What should I *do* to get sleep?" You have to "*do nothing*" to get sleep. You just need to lie down and you will drift into asleep. If you try hard to get sleep, then your very attempt to sleep will prevent you from sleeping. Otherwise, it is an effortless process. Similarly, meditation is a process in which you do not need to *do* anything. Awareness of your presence is meditation.

Whenever we are entangled in objects of the external world such as relationships, wealth, status, or power, all our senses get completely engrossed in them. Meditation, when viewed as a path, is a technique that liberates us from these external allurements and directs us within, to the experience of Self. All our senses, which are focused on the external world, should be directed to return within. This is the initial preparation for entering into meditation. The eye returns onto the eye, i.e. the eye feels or experiences itself; the ear returns onto the ear. All the senses feel and experience themselves. When the senses return onto themselves, they are then helpful for you to go within.

It is also important to understand that liberation from the external world is not the real purpose. This is only the preparation for the real purpose – Self-meditation. Due to this missing link, meditation has been restricted to the practice of sitting in solitude with closed eyes.

**Disciple: How is Self-meditation different?**

**Sirshree:** The meaning of the word meditation has been corrupted as it has been grossly misunderstood to be concentration. As a result, people focus on techniques pertaining to the body and only attain a high degree of concentration. The primary purpose behind these techniques is to stabilize in the experience of Self, followed by expression that arises from that state.

In order to refer to this original purpose without causing confusion, a new term is required. We can call it Self-meditation. Self-meditation is the experience of oneness with the Source, to be established in Self-experience. Only then is meditation focused on meditation itself.

During meditation, all kinds of thoughts arise. These thoughts torment us only because we get attached and identified with them. You are *the witness of* these thoughts. You *are not* the thoughts. When you practice detached witnessing, all the thoughts that are buried deep within you, emerge and are released. Past impressions that have impregnated mind thus gets annihilated in this process. Then Self-witnessing remains.

Knowing the Knower of all experiences in and through every experience is Self-witnessing.

Many a time, on seeing pictures of sages and saints sitting in meditation with eyes shut, it is misunderstood that they are in Self-meditation. One can never judge from the external appearance whether a person is meditating or is in the state of Self-meditation. Many people sit with closed eyes. Externally, they may appear to be in the state of Self-meditation. It is possible that they are internally filled with various thoughts of the world.

After understanding the Truth, it becomes easy for the mind to enter into the depth of meditation. Listen to the Truth, take refuge in a living Guru. Only then can you cross into the unknown without hesitation or fear. A true Guru always works upon his disciples to shift them from meditation to Self-meditation.

Self-meditation is what remains upon stabilizing in the experience of Self. Once Self-stabilization is attained, you are always in meditation; rather, you *become* Self-meditation.

### Disciple: What is the difference between *Samadhi* and meditation?

**Sirshree:** If you consider meditation from the perspective that it is to be *done*, then meditation is a path and *Samadhi* is the destination. But if you consider the real meaning of meditation, then it is an attribute of Self, just as wetness is the attribute of water.

A beginner, who does not know anything about Self will be asked to *practise* meditation to experience it. Thus, the path and the destination are taken to be different. Finally, the path itself culminates as the destination. Thus, practising meditation merely implies knowing yourself.

*Samadhi* is the ultimate goal of meditation. Every session of meditation helps in your progress. It eliminates beliefs, which act as obstacles in attaining the state of *Samadhi*. Every time you meditate on 'Who am I now?', you will receive a new insight. A new reality will dawn upon you. Each time, there will be a deeper attack on your wrong beliefs. The conviction that you are not the body will strengthen. The experience of presence will awaken. You will then be able to directly enter into the state of *Samadhi*.

When there is direct talk with truth seekers, they are told that meditation is the destination and not the path. This means meditation is the end in itself, not a means to an end.

### Disciple: Can the ultimate understanding be attained through meditation?

**Sirshree:** There is nothing outside that needs to be attained or obtained. Meditation means abiding in the Truth *within*. That Truth is not to be brought from anywhere. It has always been within us and will always be. Attaining the Truth is not difficult. After understanding the false beliefs of our mind, we begin to experience the Truth. Hence, on attaining understanding, it becomes possible to abide in the Truth. Abiding in the Truth is meditation. Thus, meditation follows *after* understanding has been attained.

It is not that meditation is done only sitting at a place. Once understanding is attained, only meditation will remain in every activity. Sitting, standing, eating, walking or working - all this will be meditation.

Hence it is said: Understand first, meditation later.

*Understanding is the seed; Meditation is the fruit.*
*Truth is the seed; Constant remembrance of God is the fruit.*

## Disciple: How is the Universal Self connected with the individual minds?

**Sirshree:** Imagine a painter who paints the picture of a paintbrush. This picture of the paintbrush comes alive and serves to create more paintings for the painter. However, if the paintbrush assumes its own individual existence and a separate personal purpose, it would go about painting without consulting the painter. Though it was created to explore and manifest the painter's creative inspiration, the paintbrush will do everything else without seeking to fulfill the painter's wish.

In the same way, the human body-mind mechanism is the Creator's creation, which serves as an instrument or medium to manifest the Creator's further creations. However, human beings perceive and operate individualistically instead of allowing the Creator to experience and express through them. Though a lot of individual and group creations may be happening in the visible realm, yet they are devoid of true and lasting contentment, since the Creator's purpose remains unfulfilled.

Let us understand this with the help of an analogy. Consider a sheet of paper on which letters are written. Each written letter contributes to the overall story that the author wishes to express. However, if any single letter were to decide to express itself differently, then will the story flow as the author intended? If a single letter were to look around the sheet and compare itself with the other letters, it may find some letters that are **bigger** in size, some that are in *italics*, some are **bolded** and hence standout. This letter may then feel dejected by comparing thus and wish that it should be like the others, or perhaps even better. However, unless the letter attains the perspective of the author or surrenders to his will, the very purpose of why it was penned on the paper is lost.

If we draw a parallel to human life, we see that individual human life is an expression on the stage of life, contributing to the overall plan of the creator. If any person gets into the game of comparison and the need for superiority and enacts such tendencies, it becomes an abnormality, a deviation to the grand plan of the creator.

We can manifest the Creator's plan only when the first creation happens first. The first creation is the act of seeking inspiration from the creator within by accessing the inner silence that exists in the background of our mind.

Paper exists between the words as well as behind them. Paper is the common substratum due to which words exist. All the words are connected at the level of the underlying paper that holds them. Every word is conveying the truth that the paper exists.

In the same way, consciousness exists within and around all bodies. All the bodies that you see around you, including your own, are enlivened by the same underlying consciousness. Everyone and everything is a serving to remind you that consciousness exists; God exists.

All the words are revealing the story of the same poet. All the words express the same reality as there is only one story being told. You need to realize that all the words only keep the story going. Bodies come and go. Their sole purpose is to keep the story of Self ongoing. Thoughts come and go. They are only conveying the truth of eternal presence.

**Disciple: This is amazing! It's really uplifting to know this higher perspective. How do I internalize it?**

**Sirshree:** You have understood it intellectually. But to truly experience it, you need to shift your perspective. Understand this with another example. There is a big pond near a mountain. You are standing at the edge of the pond and are searching for something. Someone asks you, "What do you see in the pond?" You peep into the pond and say, "I am able to see the mountain." Then the person asks again, "What else can you see?" You say, "I am able to see those birds flying in the sky." You are then told that you should not look at those objects that you have been watching so far. You are asked to start looking at that which you have not seen so far. Suddenly your focus shifts and you exclaim, "Oh yes! I am able to see *myself* in the water." You see your reflection in water, just by changing your perspective. In reality, the reflection was already there, but you were looking at everything else except your reflection.

What do you learn from this example? You only need to shift your perspective to experience your real Self. So far, you have believed yourself to be the body. Now become what you truly are. Earlier the person was looking at the pond, the mountains, birds and trees. Now he says, "I see myself in the water." His way of looking has changed. If you notice his eyes, you find that he does not need to go through any pain or effort to see himself in the world. Therefore it is said that the Truth is very simple. You only need to change your perspective. You need to behold *that* which you have not seen so far, but which has been there all the time.

### Disciple: A question on family - Do I need to renounce my family, my household to pursue Self-realization?

**Sirshree:** The belief that one should renounce one's household or relinquish one's family ties before or after Self-realization is baseless. After attaining the final understanding, one realizes that indulging in the world as a householder or renouncing the world as an ascetic are unnecessary. When both these ways are transcended, a third way called *Tej Sansari* (Bright Householder) is attained. After attaining the final understanding, you realize that a *Tej Sansari* need neither renounce nor indulge. You do not need to be a recluse; nor do you need to be engrossed in worldly pursuits. You adopt the best of both the ways and get rid of the shortcomings of both.

In the past, people were advised to relinquish everything to attain Self knowledge. Various customs were followed in earlier eras based on the need of those times. As the understanding of a person rises, it becomes easier for him to stabilize in Self-experience, even though he is engaged in the world. Saints like Guru Nanak, Saint Kabir and Saint Tukaram were established in the experience of Self while discharging the duties of a householder.

**Disciple: Is it natural to feel a different energy level and fragrance or experience the melting of the ego in the vicinity of a Self-realized soul?**

**Sirshree:** People strongly opposed saints like the Buddha, Jesus, and Meera. They were pelted with stones, crucified, or poisoned. Did those people who perpetrated such gruesome acts not experience the power, fragrance and Silence within these saints?

The fact is that only those, who have the thirst for Truth, are receptive. It is due to their receptivity that they experience the Silence, power and joy when they connect with Self-realized souls. Sunlight can stream into your house only if you open your windows. The windows of those who are not receptive remain closed. Therefore those who nurture distrust and ego cannot experience the grace in the presence of a Self-realized master.

**Disciple: Many people say that awakening of *Kundalini* leads to the vision of a thousand suns. Is this Self-realization?**

**Sirshree:** If there is a desire to experience mystical visions or bright light within, then it is like searching for the experience of Self on the body. This is the biggest hurdle in Self-realization. Whenever the experience of Self-realization is referred, the mind always attempts to experience the Self *in terms of* the mind and body. The mind always aspires to know and measure everything in its own terms. The experience of Self is the source of life. It cannot be measured or known by the mind's scale.

Experiences of the mind diminish with time. All the experiences which the mind has come across are fleeting; they exist for a short period of time and then the mind keeps yearning for them again and again. The experiences that are gained at the level of the body during meditation become an impediment in attaining Self-realization. It cannot be said for certain whether the mind or body will be able to savour the same experience again. Out of ignorance, man may repeatedly long for the same experiences at the body-mind level.

Very often, experiences that seem to be very gratifying and pleasurable to the mind are major hindrances. The sense of pure presence, of pure awareness, is the ultimate experience. You need not look for any other experience. Till now, you have believed that 'I am bound', 'I need to attain liberation'. However, as your understanding deepens, you realize that you are already liberated. Self-realization is your original nature.

Many people believe that one can behold the brightness of a thousand suns after awakening of *kundalini*. Such beliefs complicate spirituality, which is actually the simplest. Be very Awakening the *Kundalini* is only related to the body; be clear that it has nothing to do with Self-realization.

After stabilization in Self, the mind remains unshaken. When the final understanding is imparted, the essential truth of Self-realization is bestowed upon the seeker. The state of Self-realization is already present within you; you only need to realize it through experience.

**Disciple : Thanks for this profound guidance. So what is the process of Self-stabilization?**

**Sirshree :** Self-stabilization is the most important step in the journey, wherein one stabilizes in the experience of Self. One begins to constantly abide in the Truth. This involves the process called *Sadhana* – the eradication of past conditioning or programming through right understanding. The seeker remains in the presence of the Truth through constant contemplation and meditation. The mind is cleansed by uncovering the mechanical reactive patterns that are helplessly manifested through the body due to ignorance and lowered consciousness.

During the process of stabilization, the mind may get frustrated as it may not see results immediately forthcoming. The mind likes to see results instantly as per its own imaginations. The mind returns again and again with various questions, doubts and frustration about Self-experience. As a result, you may not be able to sense the Self-experience constantly. At such junctures, it is only perseverance and devotion that help in relentlessly continuing the pursuit. The doubts that are brought in by the mind should be cast aside as if they were gossiping kids who are engaged in useless chatter.

**Disciple :** Are these fluctuations an essential aspect of the journey? How do these vagaries of the mind settle?

**Sirshree :** During this journey to Self-stabilization, Self-experience may be sensed at one instant; the very next instant the sense of Self-experience may be lost. This can be compared to a bouncing ball. When you throw a ball, it goes down. But, the ball does not stay there. It bounces and rises upwards. In this way, the ball goes up before returning to the floor, only to bounce up again.

The mind also works exactly like the ball. The touching of the ball on the ground can be compared to the experience of Self. Many a time, the mind becomes disappointed believing that the experience of Self is not being felt. During this period, when you listen to the Truth in discourses, the experience is again sensed.

Every time the ball bounces, its momentum reduces. There comes a time when it stops bouncing and remains stable on the ground, at Level Zero. In the same way, depending on the body-mind makeup and the level of faith and reverence, let the mind rise and fall as many times as it will. Only then does the mind become still.

What you need to remember is that you do not need to lose hope or become agitated every time the mind rises. The experience of Self is never lost… it is always right there… behind the mind!

The experience of the Self never diminishes, although it may seem so to the mind. It is the state of the body-mind that continuously changes. The understanding that should be maintained in this situation is that we do not need to look for an 'intense' experience. The experience that you are feeling is neither less nor more. When you lead your life with this conviction, then a state will come when you will feel that even in an otherwise troublesome situation, your mind is not disturbed. The mind remains silent. As soon as the mind is silent, you will sense the awareness of Self's presence.

It is a wrong belief that we are away from the experience of Self. The final understanding is that there is no difference in the experience; it is always available to be sensed. One only needs to get rid of the belief that he is bound, or far from the Experience.

This can be achieved by listening to Truth discourses. As soon as one is rid of this belief, one realizes that he was never bound... He is already liberated from the very beginning!

**Disciple : So what is the next step?**

**Sirshree :** Understanding Self-experience intellectually is the first step. Having understood it intellectually, when you develop unshaken conviction about it, you stabilize in Self-experience. It is like one who has learnt the alphabet from A to Z, and yet does not know how to form words. You would tell him, "Since you have learned the alphabet, you will soon learn to form words."

**Disciple : I would like to learn the A to Z so as to be able to form words. How can I take the first step towards Self-stabilization?**

**Sirshree :** The Magic of Awakening retreats held here are for this purpose. You are welcome to participate.

**Disciple :  What happens in this retreat?**

**Sirshree :** The purpose of the Magic of Awakening retreat is the direct experience of Self. For clearly understanding the experience and knowing how the conviction can be raised, leading to Self-stabilization. The purpose is simply Self-experience with understanding and clarity.

You are not the body; but you are able to experience your presence due to the body. If you are able to see this clearly, then ask yourself: Why am I associated with this body? What am I doing with this body? Am I fulfilling the purpose for which I have taken up this body?

If the experience of the Self is understood, it begins to reflect in your daily life. You would then question yourself in every incident: 'What am I considering myself as in this incident?'; 'What do I believe myself to be while taking this decision?'; 'Am I considering myself to be this body, or the all-pervading consciousness that is being experienced due to the presence of the body?' When you begin to constantly remember this, then the bliss of the Self begins to deepen at the experiential level.

Let an earnest thirst emerge within you to realize the truth. May your life be driven by the highest purpose of reveling in the experience of Self and expressing its divine qualities. May you fulfil the ultimate purpose of life!

# Introduction to Sirshree

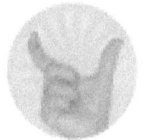

Symbol of Acceptance

Sirshree's spiritual quest which began during his childhood, led him on a journey through various schools of thought and meditation practices. The overpowering desire to attain the Truth made him relinquish his teaching job. After a long period of contemplation, his spiritual quest culminated in the attainment of the ultimate truth.

Sirshree espouses, "All paths that lead to the truth begin differently, but end in the same way—with understanding. Understanding is the whole thing. Listening to this understanding is enough to attain the truth."

He realized that the lack of Understanding was the missing link in all paths leading to Truth. He says, "Everything is a game of beliefs. Understanding is the whole thing." What he means by this (to the extent that it can be expressed in words) is that Truth has been condensed and interpreted ambiguously as a natural result of its paradoxical nature.

For instance, he says, according to one teaching, our true nature is Everythingness, while there is another teaching that refers to Nothingness as being our innate nature. Both are true, and yet the higher understanding that transcends both these teachings is that "We are Nothing with the potential of everything."

In the same vein, he goes on to expand on many traditional assertions, such as the statement, "The purpose of spiritual quest is self-realization." Sirshree says, "Self-realization is just the beginning. A true master will not just give you a glimpse. He will guide you to a state where you will be permanently established in the experience of the Self". He refers to this state as Self-stabilization. He goes further to say that Self-stabilization is not the end… it is only then that the true purpose for which your body is on Earth begins to be fulfilled. It is then that expression of the true Self begins.

To distinguish this understanding, Sirshree has coined the term *'Tej'* which literally means Bright, but which points to that which is beyond duality. For example, there is happiness, and there is unhappiness. True bliss exists beyond happiness and unhappiness. Similarly, there is ignorance, and there is knowledge. True understanding is the wisdom beyond both ignorance and knowledge. To express this, Sirshree has coined a new term called 'Knowlerience' to point to that understanding which can only be known through non-conceptual experience.

To disseminate this understanding, Sirshree devised Tejgyan—a unique system for wisdom—that helps one to progress from self-help to self-realization.

Sirshree's summation of Truth is short and concise.

- Only God (consciousness) exists. Find out whether you exist or not.
- Everything is a game of beliefs. Understanding is the whole thing.
- The purpose of life on earth is to train the mind to be unshakable, pure, obedient and loving.

- There is no other reason to be happy. The cause for happiness is always available within you.
- Guru, God, Grace, and you are one.

Sirshree has delivered more than 2000 discourses on the Truth and various aspects of practical living. Among these are discourses that clarify the core tenets of various religions. A notable assertion by Sirshree in this context is: "Mankind does not need a new religion; what it needs is the thread of understanding that can bind all religions together."

His is an amazing ability of conveying the subtlest understanding through casual contemporary language. The highest aspects of Truth are woven into analogies, parables and humor that provoke one to contemplate. Sirshree's retreats have transformed the lives of thousands and his teachings have inspired various social initiatives for raising global consciousness.

Books are one of the most far-reaching medium through which Sirshree's message touches people all over the world. Today, there are more than 70 books from Sirshree, providing guidance on a variety of subjects, be it the subject of self-realization, or complete health, the principles of karma, family harmony, true meditation, or character building.

His books have been translated in more than ten languages and published by leading publishers like Penguin, Hay House, Wisdom Tree, etc.

# TEJGYAN... THE ROAD AHEAD

## What is Tejgyan?

Tejgyan is the existential wisdom of the ultimate truth, which is beyond duality. In today's world, there are a lot of people who feel disharmony and are desperately trying to achieve some balance in an unpredictable life. Tejgyan helps them in harmonizing with their true nature, the Self, thereby restoring balance in all aspects of their life.

And then there are those who are successful but feel a sense of emptiness or void within. Tejgyan provides them fulfillment and helps them to embark on a journey towards self-realization. There are others who feel lost and are seeking the meaning of life. Tejgyan helps them to realize the true purpose of human life.

All this is possible with Tejgyan due to a very simple reason. The experience of the ultimate truth is always available. The direct experience of this truth or self-realization is possible provided the right method is known. Tejgyan is that method, that understanding. At Tej Gyan Foundation, Sirshree imparts this understanding through a System for Wisdom – a series of retreats that guides participants step by step.

## Magic of Awakening Retreat

*Magic of Awakening* is the flagship self-realization retreat offered by Tej Gyan Foundation where participants gain access to the experience of the Self and learn to live in the present every moment. The retreat is conducted in Hindi and English. The teachings of the retreat are non-denominational (secular).

Participate in the *Magic of Awakening* retreat to attain the ageless wisdom through a unique and simple 'System for Wisdom' so that you can:

1. Live from pure and still presence allowing the natural qualities of Consciousness, viz. peace, love, joy, compassion, abundance and creativity to manifest.

2. Acquire simple tools to use in everyday life which help quieten the chattering mind, revealing your true nature.

3. Get practical techniques to gain access to pure Consciousness at will and connect to the Source of all answers (the inner guru).

4. Discover the missing links in the practices of meditation (*dhyana*), action (*karma*), wisdom (*gyana)* and devotion (*bhakti*).

5. Understand the nature of your body-mind mechanism to attain freedom from tendencies and patterns.

6. Learn practical methods to shift from mind-centred living to consciousness-centred living.

This residential retreat is held for 3-5 days at the foundation's MaNaN Ashram amidst the glory of mountains and the pristine beauty of nature. This ashram is located at the outskirts of the city of Pune in India, and is well connected by air, road and rail. The retreat is also held at other centres of Tej Gyan Foundation across the world.

**For retreats in English,**
Contact +91 9011020854
Email: ma@tejgyan.com

**For retreats in Hindi,**
Contact : +91 9921008060
Email: mail@tejgyan.com

## MaNaN Ashram

Survey No. 43, Sanas Nagar, Nandoshi Gaon, Kirkatwadi Phata, Sinhagad Road, Tal. Haveli, Dist. Pune 411024, Maharashtra, India. Phone No.: 9921008060

## About Tej Gyan Foundation

Tej Gyan Foundation was established with the mission of creating a highly evolved society through all-round self development of every individual that transforms all the facets of his/her life. It is a charitable organization founded on the teachings of Sirshree. The foundation has received the ISO Certification (ISO 9001:2008) for its system of imparting wisdom. It has centres all across India as well as in other countries. The motto of Tej Gyan Foundation is 'Happy Thoughts'.

The Foundation creates a highly evolved society through:

- Tejgyan Programs (Retreats, Courses, Television and Radio Programs, Podcasts)
- Tejgyan Products (Books, Audio/Video CDs)
- Tejgyan Projects (Value Education, Women Empowerment, Peace Initiatives)

The Foundation undertakes various projects to elevate the level of consciousness among students, youth, women, senior citizens, teachers, doctors, leaders, corporates, police force, prisoners, etc.

The mission of Tej Gyan Foundation is to create a highly evolved society by raising consciousness.

- A society where individuals give top priority to Self-realization and abiding in pure consciousness.
- A society where business exist as an expression of Self.
- A society where the key department in every government is the ministry of higher consciousness.
- A society where all nationalities, races and religions co-exist happily and resolve their differences through peaceful dialogue and higher vision.

With this, we can realize limitless potential to create and transform the world into a society where:

- Importance is given to the common thread of consciousness in all religions rather than sectarian beliefs and myths of religions.
- Movies and media promote happiness, non-violence and love.
- Natural differences in men and women are cherished and each take on their unique roles.
- Children are taught how to access the peace within.
- Youth are taught how to fortify their character within kindness and compassion.

The glue that binds members of such a highly evolved society in oneness is higher consciousness.

---

**To register for the Magic of Awakening Retreat, contact:**

**Pune Centre** : Vikrant Complex, Near Tapovan Mandir, Pimpri, Pune – 411017

Telephone: 020-67097700, 09921008060/75, 09011013208

---

Books can be delivered at your doorstep by registered post or courier. You can request for the same through postal money order or pay by VPP. Please send the money order to:

Tejgyan Global Foundation, Pimpri Colony, P. O. Box 25, Pimpri, Pune – 411017 (Maharashtra) Mobile: 09011013210

Postage fee will not be charged when you order books by post.

You may also avail of 10% discount if you order more than 4 books at the same time.

You can also order the books online at www.gethappythoughts.org

## For Further Details Contact :

### TEJGYAN GLOBAL FOUNDATION
P.O. Box No. 25, Pimpri Colony Post Office, Pune 411017, Maharashtra, India.

### MaNaN Ashram :
Survey No. 43, Sanas Nagar, Nandoshi gaon, Kirkatwadi Phata, Sinhagad Road, Tal. Haveli, Dist. Pune 411024, Maharashtra, India.
Contact No.: 992100 8060.

### Registered Office :
Happy Thoughts Building, Vikrant Complex, Near Tapovan Mandir, Pimpri, Pune 411 017, Maharashtra, India.

For accessing our unique 'System for Wisdom'
from Self-help to Self-realization, please follow us on:

|  | Website | www.tejgyan.org |
|---|---|---|
|  | Book and events micro-site | www.thesourcebook.org |
|  | Online shopping / Blog | www.gethappythoughts.org |
|  | Video Channel | www.youtube.com/tejgyan |
|  | Email | mail@tejgyan.com |
|  | Social networking | www.facebook.com/tejgyan |
|  | Social networking | www.twitter.com/sirshree |
|  | Social networking | google.com/+TejgyanOrganisation |
|  | Social networking blog | http://www.speakingtree.in/thetejgyan.ofsirshree |

Please pray for World Peace along with thousands of others at 09:09 a.m. and p.m. every day.

### Discourses of Sirshree
24x7 Tejgyan Internet Radio : http://www.tejgyan.org/internetradio.aspx
Mon to Sat 6.35 to 6.55 p.m., Sun 8:10 to 8:30 p.m. on Sanskar TV Channel
*(These timings may be subject to change.)*

www.ingramcontent.com/pod-product-compliance
Lightning Source LLC
LaVergne TN
LVHW040201080526
838202LV00042B/3259